MW01105431

Daddy is a
Conundrum!

BY DR. N. TRAN-DAVIES
ILLUSTRATED BY STEPHANIE PARKER

Produced by:

 **Friesen Press**

Suite 300 – 852 Fort Street
Victoria, BC, Canada V8W 1H8
www.friesenpress.com

Distributed to the trade by The Ingram Book Company

Dedicated to GKMS and Ronnie.

Proceeds will go towards cancer research.

Mr. **EiNSTeiN** states $E=MC^2$

Rather **eLeMeNtary,** we declare.

Compared to Daddy's **Scraggly** beard.

Short or long, it's just a little **Weird**.

A whiskery curl to his chin from his nose

Prickly, tickly however it grows.

Daddy's a CONUNDRUM!

$a^2 + b^2 = c^2$ does

Mr. **PyтHagoraS** announce

Most **rudiMeNtary**, we pronounce.

Compared to Daddy's
curious, raucous sounds

With snores that **rattle and shake**

the grounds.

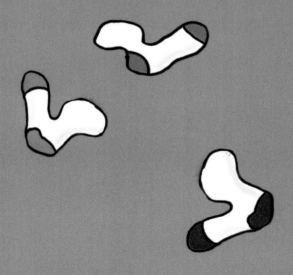

And horns and flutes that often **Hoot**

Somewhat **SMeLLy** with every **toot**.

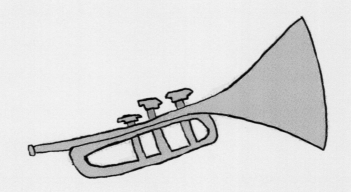

Daddy's a CONUNDRUM!

13

Then there's Mr. NeWToN'S Gravity LaW

Quite the tHeory, if an apple did fall.

More **PERPLEXING** are

Daddy's **racKety** skills

Making or **breaKiNG** whatever he will.

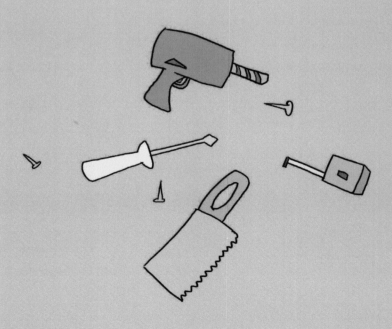

With two left hands and two left feet

CLANGING BANGING, stepping and **STOMPING**, to whatever his beat.

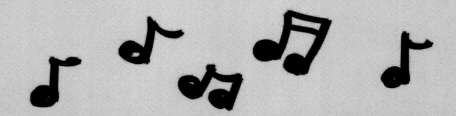

Daddy's a CONUNdrUM!

When Mr. **GaLiLeo** insists
the **SUN** is central.

'Twas a **revolutionary,**
orbital spectacle.

Much like Daddy's **tall, tall** tales

Stories of **treasures**

like the Holy Grail.

Of **StReNgtH** to cast a
hundred **giaNtS** aside

Yet gentle is he, drying the tears we cried.

Daddy's a CONUNdrUM!

We **evolved**, Mr. **DarWiN** does write

SiMPLy PriMary, with us

monkeys in sight.

How **evolutionary** when

Daddy sees our fine, fine mess

With scribbled walls, shattered glass,

broken rules… **We coNFeSS!**

Yet he holds us **Wiggly**

Gigglies tight

To love his **Turkey Lurkies**

with all his might!

Oh! Daddy is a CONUNDRUM!

CPSIA information can be obtained
at www.ICGtesting.com
Printed in the USA
LVIC090750101112
306616LV00004BB